Hats Can Help

The Sound of H

By Alice K. Flanagan

The Child's World®, Inc.

Hats can help if the sun is too hot.

Hats can help if you are in the sun or not.

4

Hats can help if things get bad.

Hats can help if you
are sad.

Hats can help when you play ball.

Hats can help if you fall.

12

14

Hats can help you if things fall.

Hats can help you
know who to call.

18

Hats can help if you are baking buns.

Hats can help you to have fun.

Word List

hats

have

help

hot

Note to Parents and Educators

The books in the Phonics series of the Wonder Books are based on current research which supports the idea that our brains are pattern detectors rather than rules appliers. This means children learn to read easier when they are taught the familiar spelling patterns found in English. As children encounter more complex words, they have greater success in figuring out these words by using the spelling patterns.

Throughout the 35 books, the texts provide the reader with the opportunity to practice and apply knowledge of the sounds in natural language. The 10 books on the long and short vowels introduce the sounds using familiar onsets and rimes, or spelling patterns, for reinforcement. For example, the word "cat" might be used to present the short "a" sound, with the letter "c" being the onset and "-at" being the rime. This approach provides practice and reinforcement of the short "a" sound, as there are many familiar words made with the "-at" rime.

The 21 consonants and the 4 blends ("ch," "sh," "th," and "wh") use many of these same rimes. The letter(s) before the vowel in a word are considered the onset. Changing the onset allows the consonant books in the series to maintain the practice and reinforcement of the rimes. The repeated use of a word or phrase reinforces the target sound.

The number on the spine of each book facilitates arranging the books in the order that children acquire each sound. The books can also be arranged into groups of long vowels, short vowels, consonants, and blends. All the books in each grouping have their numbers printed in the same color on the spine. The books can be grouped and regrouped easily and quickly, depending on the teacher's needs.

The stories and accompanying photographs in this series are based on time-honored concepts in children's literature: Well-written, engaging texts and colorful, high-quality photographs combine to produce books that children want to read again and again.

Dr. Peg Ballard
Minnesota State University, Mankato

Photo Credits

All photos © copyright: Dembinsky Photo Associates: 2 (Robert Sisk), 5 (Stephen Graham), 6 (John Mielcarek), 13 (Mark E. Gibson), 17 (Stephen J. Shaluta Jr.); PhotoEdit: 21 (Richard Hutchings); Photri Inc.: 14 (Gatzen); Tony Stone Images: 9 (Steven Weinberg), 18 (Don Smetzer); Unicorn Stock Photos: 10 (Robert W. Ginn). Cover: Tony Stone/Gary Holschen.

Photo Research: Alice Flanagan
Design and production: Herman Adler Design Group

Library of Congress Cataloging-in-Publication Data

Flanagan, Alice K.
    Hats can help : the sound of "h" / by Alice K. Flanagan.
      p. cm. — (Wonder books)
    Summary : Simple text and repetition of the letter "h" help readers learn how to use this sound.
    ISBN 1-56766-693-0 (lib. bdg. : alk. paper)
    [1. Hats Fiction. 2. Alphabet. 3. Stories in rhyme.] I. Title. II. Series: Wonder books (Chanhassen, Minn.)
PZ8.3.F6365Hat   1999
[E]—dc21
                                       99-20961
                                         CIP